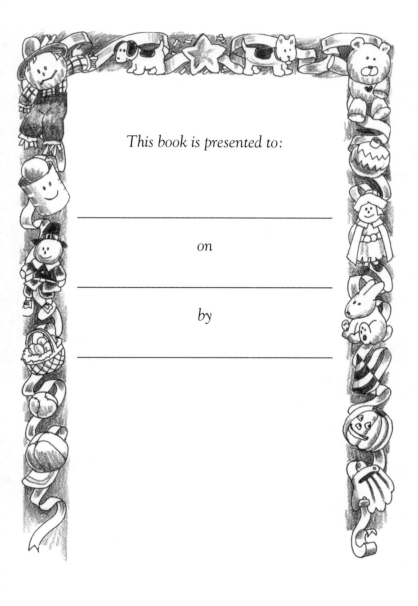

This book is presented to:

---

on

---

by

Adventures at the Grandparents' House

Marge Alexander

Illustrated by Joe McCormick

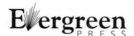

Evergreen PRESS

Adventures at the Grandparents' House
by Marge Alexander

ISBN 1-58169-064-9
Printed in the U.S.A.
For Worldwide Distribution

Evergreen Press
P.O. Box 91011 • Mobile, AL 36691
800-367-8203

TABLE OF CONTENTS

ACKNOWLEDGEMENTS

With special thanks to
Kim, Sue, and Jim,
without whom there could not have been
grandchildren;
and to the faithful friends who read my stories,
believed they were valuable,
and spurred me on.

INTRODUCTION

The stories in *Adventures at the Grandparents' House* came about quite by accident. Our oldest daughter and her family live overseas. As each holiday approached, I would send a book which talked about it. We were anxious for our grandchildren to have a real sense of the way holidays are celebrated in America. It was important to us that they know our traditions and understand their heritage.

On one particular holiday, I realized that there wasn't time to send a book and have it arrive for the holiday. So I decided to write a story and e-mail it to them. To my delight, not only did I thoroughly enjoy writing the story, the grandchildren loved it and asked for more.

One thing led to another, and I began to write a story for each of our children and their families and for each holiday. Each of the characters in the book actually did live (some would say "were in storage") on the shelves in our basement. I do admit that none of them could actually talk, but each one is bursting with stories to tell if they only could.

I believe that it is important to pass traditions on to the next generation. So it brings us joy to see each of our children and their families now carrying on our traditions, and even building new ones of their own.

It is my desire that grandparents, parents, aunts, uncles, and friends will read these stories with young ones with whom they want to make memories and be blessed.

DEDICATION

These stories are dedicated to the memory of my mother, whose time with me was far too brief, but who I know prayed for me for the five years we had together.

And I dedicate this book to my dear husband who encouraged me to put these memories down on paper.

And this book is especially dedicated to:

The Grandchildren!

Chapter One

ABRAHAM, THE FAITHFUL SCARECROW

Deep in the basement of the grandparents' house stood a large set of wooden shelves. On them the grandparents kept all the holiday decorations and ornaments they had collected over the years. Some were in boxes, some were in large plastic bags, and others were set directly on the shelves, but each one had its own special place and was brought upstairs only at certain times of the year.

No one could remember where Abraham the scarecrow had come from...the grandparents weren't even sure how many years they had set him out at harvest time. They knew they must have gotten him a long time ago. He seemed to have always been part of their Fall decorations and always had a place on the shelves deep in the basement of the grandparents' house.

This particular harvest season, the grandmother considered getting rid of old Abraham. He was rather tattered looking, and besides, he didn't smell very good. His straw filling had gathered lots of dust over the years and his clothes had faded. His old hat had begun to fray, and the feather in his hat was bare in some parts. He wore a vest and blue trousers with a piece of yarn around his waist which served as a belt. His eyes, nose and mouth that were made of felt, now sagged, giving him more of a frown than a smile on his face. Bits of straw stuck out from the sleeves of his shirt and the legs of his pants. It was true, he wasn't much to look at and he didn't smell very good, but still, the grandmother just couldn't bring herself to throw him away.

Instead, she decided to clean him up. The grandmother began by brushing off the dust and fixing the straw that made Abraham strong and tall. Next, she replaced his old torn clothes with a beautiful, bright set of new ones and put a perky hat on his head with a brand new feather on the side. She even cut out new bits of felt to make him smile instead of frown. Finally she sprayed some nice smelling spray on him. He looked like a brand new scarecrow and had never been more handsome!

As the grandmother hung old Abraham up, she had to chuckle to herself when she looked at the smile on his face. She wondered if he really was as happy as that smile seemed to make him look.

Many of Abraham's relatives and friends were not as fortunate as he was. Most of them had to stand outside in fields to keep the crows away from crops. Others stood on porches and some leaned against fences or lampposts to herald the coming of Fall and the harvest season which was underway. He got to live in a cozy warm basement most of the year, and the rest of the time he was set out as a decoration in the grandparents' house. He must have delighted in seeing the grandchildren come and go during the Fall season.

The grandmother decided to rest after she finished putting all the harvest decorations out, each in its own very special place. All that work always made the grandmother tired and ready for a nice hot cup of tea. So she went to the kitchen, brewed a cup of her favorite peppermint tea, and sat in the rocking chair by the window to relax.

The grandmother sipped her tea and looked out the window at the leaves dancing around the yard in the gentle Fall breeze. She was deep in thought as she remembered the children when they were little and how they loved to run and play. She remembered how they enjoyed raking the leaves into one huge pile and then jumped in it. They would often hide in the leaves and wait for someone to come looking for them. They took great delight in jumping out of the leaves, roaring like a lion and scaring the poor person half to death!

As the grandmother was deep in thought, she was startled to hear what sounded like someone clearing his throat. "Excuse me," she heard someone say. (Now, it's important to remember that grandparents can hear things that other people can't.) She was so startled that she almost spilled her cup of tea. She turned around to see where the voice was coming from. She could hardly believe it, but the voice was coming from Abraham!

Can you imagine how surprised the grandmother must have been? She could hardly believe her ears. It's true that she had often spoken with the other decorations, but old Abraham had hung there in the entryway for years, and never said one single word. The grandmother thought he was one decoration who just didn't speak. Well, she was wrong, Abraham just had waited until he had something to say!

"Excuse me," he said a second time. "I have hung here for many years, watching the children grow and now watching those wonderful grandchildren. I had a feeling that you were going to throw me away this year, and I wanted to thank you for not doing that. I am very grateful for the new set of clothes and the new smile that you gave me. I feel like a whole new scarecrow!"

Once the grandmother realized that Abraham could talk, you can just imagine all the questions she wanted to ask him! Where did he come from, how old was he, why did he suddenly decide to speak? Here is what Abraham told her…

Once, long ago, Abraham was a handsome fresh-smelling young scarecrow. He hung in a roadside stand with many of his relatives. He loved being where he could see the cars go by and lots of people come into the roadside stand to buy fruits and vegetables. Occasionally, someone would buy one of Abraham's relatives. Abraham couldn't remember how long he lived at the roadside stand. One day a young man came in and saw Abraham. He looked him over very carefully; he walked all around him; he even inspected how Abraham was put together. Finally, he told the owner of the roadside stand that he wanted to buy Abraham.

The man took Abraham home with him, but the strangest thing happened—Abraham was left in the box! It was put into a dark room, and he never again saw the man who bought him. Abraham could not tell how long he lived all alone in that cold, dark box. It was very hard for Abraham; he missed all the excitement and the people at the roadside stand.

One day when Abraham had given up hope of ever being around people again, something wonderful happened. Suddenly the box, which by now was old and musty smelling, was carried out into the sunlight and opened up. Abraham was almost blinded by the light. He couldn't imagine what was happening!

Abraham found himself piled on a table with an odd assortment of things. There were clothes, dishes, toys, and many other things that Abraham couldn't identify. He was frightened because he had no idea where he was, or why people were picking him up and dropping him back down. It was all very upsetting to poor Abraham.

After awhile, a lovely lady picked Abraham up. She looked at Abraham with kind eyes and handled him ever so gently, more gently than Abraham had ever been treated. Suddenly he was no longer frightened, and he no longer felt alone or sad. When she brought him home, he knew that he was going to begin a wonderful new life. It wasn't long after meeting this lovely lady that he found himself on the shelves deep in the basement of the grandparents' house.

Abraham had so many things he wanted to tell the grandmother. First of all, he told her how he was so happy to have finally been cleaned up; he hadn't liked the way he looked or even worse, the way he smelled. But there was nothing he could do about it himself! He enjoyed the fresh straw inside, his new set of clothes, and especially the bright smile on his face. That is why Abraham decided to speak. He felt brand new—he was clean inside and out, and he just couldn't keep that kind of happiness to himself.

As the grandmother sat drinking her tea and thinking about everything Abraham had said, she thought about all God had done for her. It was very much like what she had done for Abraham.

God had come come into her life when she was lost and very frightened. He healed her broken heart and forgave her sins. His love made her new and clean; she smelled sweet to her Father in heaven. He put a smile on her face and adopted her into His family, just as the grandmother had brought Abraham home long ago and made him part of her family. The grandmother was filled with joy when she thought about all the wonderful things that God had done for her.

The grandmother slowly sipped her peppermint tea, lovingly looked at Abraham, and counted her blessings.

Chapter Two

BARNABAS, THE ENCOURAGING BEAR

Long ago, before there were shelves deep in the basement of the grandparents' house, there was a little boy who would one day grow up to be the grandfather.

One day the boy's father came home from work with something hidden in his jacket. He had a big smile on his face, and his jacket seemed to be alive with movement. The boy and his two older sisters watched with excitement as the father asked them to guess what it was. The children squealed with delight as they tried very hard to guess. Could it be a kitten? Maybe it was a bunny rabbit, maybe…could it be a puppy?

That was it! The father opened his jacket and out popped the most wonderful puppy the little boy had ever seen. The little boy was delighted with the puppy. It jumped and ran, chased its tail, and covered the little boy's face with wet kisses. The puppy was brown with white spots all over its body. After lots of thought and discussion, the family decided to name the dog "Rex."

Rex became a constant companion of the little boy. The sisters played with Rex, too, but nobody loved him quite as much as the little boy. They ran through the fields together; they played fetch; but most of all they just loved each other. The sisters went to school each day, but the little boy was not old enough yet, so he and Rex spent long days doing all the things that boys and dogs love to do together.

One day Rex was outside all alone when a big, mean dog came running into the yard. Rex was very trusting and ran up to the strange dog to make friends. Before Rex knew what happened, the big dog bit him. The family heard Rex's cries and ran out into the yard. Rex was bleeding and badly hurt. The father and mother gently carried Rex into the house and cleaned and bandaged his wounds. The mother wrapped poor

Rex in a blanket and laid him gently by the warm fireplace. The father sat with Rex while the mother tucked the little boy and his sisters into bed.

Morning came and the children hurried out of bed to see how Rex was doing. As the three children ran into the kitchen, they found the father sitting in his chair with tears in his eyes, but Rex was nowhere to be seen. The children knew, without being told, that Rex had not been able to survive the wounds inflicted by the big, mean dog.

The days after Rex died were very sad days for the little boy and his family. They were especially difficult for the little boy. The mother tried hard to think of things for the little boy to do, but it seemed that nothing helped him stop missing his dear friend Rex.

One night after he was asleep, the mother and father talked about how sad their little boy was. They wondered what they could do to bring the smile back to his little face. They finally came up with a plan to help the little boy be happy again.

The next day the father came home from work, but he didn't take off his jacket as he usually did. Instead he stood in the kitchen with his arms wrapped in front of him and called the little boy.

The father looked down at him with a twinkle in his eye and said, "Son, I have something for you in my jacket."

The little boy couldn't imagine what it could be. The jacket didn't move like it did when his father brought Rex home. *What,* he wondered, *could my father possibly have under his jacket?*

The father opened his jacket, and there was the most amazing stuffed bear the little boy had ever seen. He was light brown with big, black button eyes that seemed to look right into the little boy's heart. He had a little soft nose and two big fluffy ears so he could hear everything the boy had to say. He had a little thread mouth which seemed to smile with delight when the boy came near for a closer look. The most important thing the bear had (which only the little boy could see) was a big heart that longed to encourage the boy and make him happy again.

The little boy reached into his father's jacket and pulled the bear into his arms; he hugged the bear ever so tight. Then the boy looked up at his mother and father and asked, "Does the bear have a name?" They told him that indeed the bear did have a name—his name was Barnabas which means *encouragement.* She went on to tell the little boy that Barnabas had a very special job to do, and that job was to encourage the little boy and to help him be happy again.

Barnabas was a wonderful bear. He loved to nuzzle the little boy with his soft little nose when the boy held him close. Barnabas especially loved to listen to the little boy with his big fluffy ears. The little boy told Barnabas all about his dog Rex and the fun he had with him. He could almost see Barnabas' little mouth smile. Most of all, Barnabas loved the boy with his big heart, and oh, how that encouraged the little boy! He knew Barnabas had the perfect name.

Each day the little boy got Barnabas and off they would go together. Barnabas loved to be with the little boy when he was playing with his trucks in the sandbox or drawing pictures at the kitchen table. Barnabas especially enjoyed the times when the mother read stories to the little boy. Barnabas was a happy bear because he knew that he was an encouragement to his little friend.

The years went by and the little boy grew, as boys do, until he was old enough to go to school. The boy kissed his mother goodbye, and he kissed his good friend Barnabas goodbye and gently laid him on his bed. The day seemed very long to Barnabas while he waited for his little friend to return.

Finally Barnabas heard the sound of children's voices downstairs and knew that the boy was finally home. It wasn't long before the boy came bounding up the stairs into the bedroom to tell Barnabas all about his day at school. Barnabas was glad to hear about the boy's day, but most of all he was happy to have his friend home again. Each day went pretty much the same, and Barnabas liked it that way.

The years went by, and as the boy grew he spent less and less time playing the way small boys play. Now after school, the father allowed him to come out to the farm where the boy enjoyed spending time in the barn with the animals. When the boy became a teenager, he had a lot of fun raising a cow from a calf. He spent even less time in his room. Poor old Barnabas missed all the attention the boy used to give to him. Each morning when the boy made his bed he would put old Barnabas in his special place right in the center. But that was all the time he spent with Barnabas.

When the boy became a young man, he decided to go off and join the Army. As he packed his bags, he noticed his old friend Barnabas laying on his bed as he had for so many years. Before he left, the young man picked him up and told him about the grand new adventure that was about to begin. Barnabas wished he could go with him but knew that it wasn't possible. Barnabas was a very sad bear. He didn't feel he could possibly live up to his name and be an encouragement to anyone; in fact, he felt like he was the one who needed of encouragement!

Many years went by...Barnabas lay alone on the boy's bed, and it seemed that everyone had just about forgotten him. Occasionally the boy's mother would come into the room. When she did, she would pick up poor old Barnabas and together they would think about how much they both missed the little boy who was all grown up and living in a far away land. It was a sad and lonely time for the bear who used to be so happy.

Barnabas didn't look quite as handsome as he did when the boy first saw him on that day long ago. His light brown fur was faded and there were places where some of it was missing. He lost one of his black button eyes and even one of his big fluffy ears. Those fluffy ears had heard so many things over the years! However, one thing had not changed. Barnabas still had a heart that was full of love for the boy who seemed to have forgotten all about him.

Several people came into the boy's room one day and began packing things into boxes. Barnabas was glad to have company; he got very lonely in that room all by himself. Before he knew what had happened, someone put him into a box and placed the lid on it. And that is where he stayed for a long, long time. Poor Barnabas lost all hope of ever being happy again. He felt like just an old, worn-out stuffed bear.

Then one day, the box was opened! There were voices all around him, and he couldn't tell who any of them belonged to. As he was lifted up from the box, he looked into the face of someone who seemed very familiar. Barnabas suddenly realized that it was the boy who had grown up to be a man! The man, now a father, told his children how much he loved Barnabas, and how Barnabas had encouraged him and helped him to be happy when his heart broke so many years ago.

The children thought Barnabas was a wonderful bear. They didn't mind that his fur was faded and worn, they didn't mind that he was missing an eye and an ear. They saw that he had something far more important — a heart filled with love.

Barnabas was gently placed on a bed in the children's room. He watched them play and listened to all the wonderful stories they had to tell, and even the boy who had grown up to be a father would often come into the room and say hello to his old friend Barnabas.

Barnabas was a very happy bear once again. For many years, he lived in the house that is now the grandparents' house. Barnabas learned that when he thought he had been forgotten and forsaken there was joy and usefulness just around the corner.

Barnabas now lives with some of the grandchildren who are moving to a new town where they will have to make new friends. Barnabas knows all about feeling lonely, and he is ready to love them with his big, old heart and help them with all the changes. He will happily listen to the stories that the children will tell him because he is still anxious to be the Bear of Encouragement.

Chapter Three

AMOS, THE PARTY PUMPKIN

There were several pumpkins who lived on one of the lower shelves deep in the basement of the grandparents' house. On the far left was a pumpkin made of ceramic who lived in a padded box because he was so very fragile. Next to him there were several little pumpkins who lay all jumbled in a small box because they were only made of plastic (although they were special to the grandparents, too). Then there was Amos—the biggest pumpkin of them all, and so he sat directly on the shelf. He wasn't made of ceramic; he wasn't made of plastic; he was made of a fuzzy kind of material. Amos was different from all the other pumpkins—he had a light inside him and, therefore, a special job to do. His job was to light the front of the house at harvest time.

Every year Amos could hardly wait for the cooler weather to come. It was then that the grandparents would bring him and all the other Fall decorations upstairs to the main part of the house and put each one in a special place for the harvest season.

As soon as the season had passed and Amos was put back on his basement shelf, he began to dream about the next year when he and his friends would be brought out again. The first holiday that passed was Thanksgiving. Amos could smell turkey cooking and hear busy footsteps over his head up in the main part of the house. He knew it would be a long time before he would get back out to light the front of the house again.

Then came the Christmas season. He watched the grandparents come for the tree, the special Christmas angel, the nativity set, and all the decorations that were used to celebrate the birth of the Christ Child. How he wished he was going with them! He heard the Christmas music and the guests arriving. He heard carolers come by and sing their holiday songs, but all he could do was sit there and wait…and listen.

Then came the New Year and after that all the decorations from the Christmas holiday came back to live on the basement shelves with him. The Christmas decorations told about all the wonderful sights that they saw and what fun they had while they were upstairs.

It was always a long, lonely winter for all the decorations who lived on the shelves deep in the basement of the grandparents' house. Finally, Amos could tell that the weather was changing because it was getting warmer downstairs where he and his friends lived. "It must be Spring!" Amos told his friends. The air smelled different now.

One day the grandparents came downstairs and began to look through the decorations. Amos wondered hopefully, *Could it be Fall already?* Were they coming for him and his friends? Amos was a little sad when he saw the grandparents take the Easter decorations upstairs, but he knew that the time was getting closer when the grandparents would come for him and his friends once again.

It wasn't long after the Easter decorations had returned to their shelf when something began happening in the upper part of the house. Amos heard a lot of excitement from the grandparents. There was much moving of furniture and lots of activity that Amos had never heard before. "What could be happening?" Amos asked his friends.

One day the grandparents and their friends were down in the room near where Amos and the other decorations lived. He heard them talking about someone coming for a visit. *Who could it be?* they wondered. Then Amos heard the grandparents say that some of the grandchildren who lived a long way off were coming for a visit. Amos was so excited he could hardly stand it! He and the other decorations had long talks about how much fun it would be to have grandchildren around while they were out decorating the house. Adults like decorations, but nobody really appreciates them as much as the grandchildren. How exciting this was going to be!

The rainy season turned into dry, hot days and the grandchildren arrived. Oh, what excitement filled the house! The sound of the children's laughter and running footsteps could be heard all day long. Amos' place on the shelf was just right so that even when the grandchildren played outside he could hear them on the swings and in the swimming pool. Amos could hardly wait until it was time for him to be out so that he could be with the grandchildren!

The summer season was finally over and Amos' favorite time of the year was coming soon. He heard the grandparents talking about how beautiful the colors of the leaves were this year. He saw that the days were getting shorter and the nights were getting cooler. "Surely," Amos told his friends, "it's almost time for us to be put on display!"

The happy day arrived. The grandparents came downstairs and gathered all the harvest decorations.

They put the fragile ceramic pumpkin on the big windowsill in the dining room. Around it they put the little plastic pumpkins along with red and orange and yellow leaves. Then the grandfather took Amos and hung him by the front door—the most important place of all—so he could light the way in the early darkness.

As soon as Amos was hung out front, he looked all around. *Where are the grandchildren?* he wondered. *Surely they will be here soon.* He waited and waited. Amos began to feel quite sad; he had thought that he would hang in front of the house and see the grandchildren run and play and wave and shout happy hellos to him. But he thought, *I guess I shall have to wait a while longer.*

Then Amos heard children walking up and down the street in front of the grandparents' house. *Could it be the grandchildren?* he wondered. He kept listening for the young voices he had heard during the summer at the grandparents' house, but they didn't come. Day after day, Amos became more and more sad. Something began to happen to him—his covering began to look faded and sunken and his smile wasn't so big any more. He wondered what could have happened to the grandchildren, *Why don't they come to see me and watch me while I light the way here in front of the house?*

One day when the grandparents were outside, they looked up at Amos, and the grandmother asked, "Look, Grampa, is that a tear I see on Amos' face?"

They wondered why he looked so sad and faded.

He had always been a brightly colored, smiling pumpkin.

"What's wrong, Amos?" asked the grandmother.

(Now, it's very important to understand that grandparents can sometimes hear sounds that no one else can hear.) Amos told them that he had expected this year to be special. He had heard the grandchildren playing and laughing on their visits and was looking forward to seeing them. Amos told them that he had wanted to make this a special harvest season for the grandchildren, but they didn't come and so he was very sad.

The grandparents now understood why there were tears in Amos' eyes and why he was looking so faded and sad. They felt almost as bad as Amos because the grandchildren were far away and could not enjoy the harvest season with them.

That night, the grandparents had an idea. Through the front screen door, Amos heard lots of laughter and planning going on between the grandparents. The next morning, the grandfather took Amos from the front porch and hung him in a place that Amos had never been before—the garage. The grandfather patted Amos gently, closed the door, and went away. Amos was left hanging there feeling alone and cold and more unhappy than ever. He thought maybe he was put away in the dark because he didn't look as good as he used to look.

Later that day, Amos heard the grandparents and their friends coming to the garage. They opened the door, turned on all the lights (including Amos), and began to hang up lovely, bright decorations that Amos met for the first time. Amos felt a little embarrassed because he looked so faded.

Suddenly Amos heard the sound of children's voices, voices that he had never heard before. They weren't the voices of the grandchildren from far away; they weren't the voices of the children that Amos knew lived near the grandparents; these were new voices, many happy excited ones.

Amos could hardly believe his eyes—he was right in the middle of a harvest party! He learned that these were the grandchildren of the grandparents' friends who lived nearby! How happy he was! There were games for the children to play; there was much wonderful food to eat; but, best of all, there was laughter and joy all around him. Amos realized that when he was hung in the garage earlier that day, he was not put in a place where no one would see him as he had thought. The grandfather hung him where he would be right in the middle of the wonderful party so that he could shine his light down on all the fun. He realized that even though he was no longer as handsome as he once was, the grandparents still loved him and wanted to use him!

Amos suddenly felt something strange happening to him. He hadn't really noticed when he was grumpy and sad on the inside that he had also become faded and sunken on the outside. But suddenly he knew that now he was just as plump and smiling as before, and the light that shone out from inside of him was brighter than he ever remembered it.

Amos learned a very important lesson that day. He learned that when we get disappointed, it can really make us quite sad. He also learned that just because it looks like we have been forgotten, we still need to trust those who are taking care of us. There might just be something wonderful around the corner.

Amos needed to trust the grandparents, but real people need to trust God. They need to trust that He knows all about the disappointments in their lives. Even when they can't see it or feel it, He is still working things out for their good.

Chapter Four

AARON AND ABIGAIL, PILGRIMS WITH A PURPOSE

It was that time of year at the grandparents' house when Amos the pumpkin had to go back to the shelves deep in the basement. It was also the time of year when the grandparents would display the Thanksgiving decorations. They would bring Ezra, the noble Thanksgiving turkey, upstairs along with the basket filled with different fruits and vegetables and brightly colored leaves. They set out candles and flowers to make it all very bright and colorful. As the grandfather stood back, looking at the display, he thoughtfully stroked his chin.

"Grandma," the grandfather said, "there is something missing from our Thanksgiving decorations."

The grandmother couldn't figure out what was missing—these were the same decorations they had been putting on display for many years. So what could possibly be missing?

The grandfather suddenly said, "Pilgrims! That's what's missing. We need to find some pilgrims."

The grandmother immediately agreed, and so the search began. The grandparents went looking for pilgrims, but not just any pilgrims, these had to be special ones.

The grandfather didn't know exactly what he was looking for in these pilgrims, but he told the grandmother, "When we see them, we will know they are the right ones."

The grandparents went to many different stores: they went to gift shops; they went to department stores; they went to malls; and they even looked in catalogs for the special pilgrims. They saw many different ones. Some were too big, and some were too small. Some were perfectly lovely pilgrims, but the grandparents just couldn't seem to find the ones that they knew would be just right for them. The grandmother told the grandfather that maybe they wouldn't be able to find just the right ones this year, but the grandfather was determined to keep looking until they found them.

One day they walked into one of their favorite stores. As they looked at all the wonderful decorations, they finally saw just what they had been searching for! There, right in the center of the display were the perfect pilgrims, Aaron and Abigail. Aaron stood holding a pumpkin, and a basket of wheat was beside him. Abigail had a basket of fruit by her side and in her arms she held some flowers. Aaron had a pilgrim hat on his head, and he was very handsome. Abigail was wearing a long dress and apron and a pretty bonnet on her head. She had a warm friendly smile on her round little face.

The grandparents knew immediately that these were the pilgrims they had been looking for, although they couldn't explain exactly why. They looked at each other with a smile that said, "These are the ones!" The grandfather picked up Aaron, and the grandmother picked up Abigail, and they brought them over to the checkout counter.

Now Aaron and Abigail had been quite happy to be displayed in the store, standing proudly in the center of it all. They liked watching the people shop, and they enjoyed getting to know all the other decorations. Aaron and Abigail were not at all sure they were pleased about what was happening to them now.

The clerk in the store wrapped Aaron and Abigail

carefully in soft paper, placed them gently in a box, and off they went with the grandparents. So began the wonderful adventure for Aaron and Abigail.

At first Aaron and Abigail felt frightened about where they might be going, but they knew that they should be brave because, after all, they were pilgrims. They were supposed to remind everyone of the brave people who had come to America hundreds of years ago. But, at the moment, they didn't feel very brave at all.

After what seemed to Aaron and Abigail like a very long time, the grandparents began to unwrap them from their soft paper. They lovingly set the two pilgrims on a special table in front of a mirror. There were lots of other decorations in the room as well, although not nearly as many as Aaron and Abigail were used to seeing in the store.

The first decoration they met was Ezra the big beautiful turkey who later became one of their best friends. The pilgrims decided that the basket with the leaves, fruits, and vegetables spilling out of it was quite beautiful. And they admired the scented candles and fresh flowers that smelled so pretty. It was all quite lovely to look at, and Aaron and Abigail finally felt content to be part of this Thanksgiving display.

After the grandparents had put the finishing touches on the arrangement, they stood back and talked about how perfect Aaron and Abigail looked and how well they fit in with all the other decorations.

The grandparents knew that they had found the perfect pilgrims to stand in that special place in front of the dining room mirror.

It was almost Thanksgiving, and there was much for the grandparents to do. There was a flurry of excitement going on in the kitchen next to the dining room. The grandmother was very busy with all the baking that grandmothers do at this special time of the year. There was the turkey to stuff and roast. (Ezra was so grateful that he was safe and would never be stuffed and roasted!) There were pies, cakes, and rolls to bake, and all the vegetables to peel and wash in preparation for the big day. The smells were more wonderful than anything Aaron and Abigail had ever experienced when they lived on the department store's shelves.

The most exciting part of living in the grandparents' house was yet to come. Soon it was Thanksgiving morning. Aaron and Abigail heard sounds that they hadn't heard since they had come to live in the grandparents' house. They heard children laughing and squealing as they came running, jumping, and bouncing into the dining room. The children all stopped at once when they saw the pilgrims in front of the mirror.

"New decorations!" they shouted, as they struggled to get a really good look at Aaron and Abigail.

The pilgrims wondered if they were safe with all these little people excitedly pushing around so close to them. They were relieved when the grandparents began to explain to the grandchildren how fragile they were.

Aaron and Abigail began to feel very special as they listened to the grandparents tell how they had searched in so many stores before they had found them.

Finally it was time for the whole family to sit down at the bountiful table for Thanksgiving dinner. The grandfather asked each person to name a special blessing that he or she was thankful for. It was important, the grandparents explained, to remember that this wasn't just a day to eat turkey and have fun together, but that most importantly, it was a day to thank God for all the blessings He had given to each of them over the past year.

He smiled at Aaron and Abigail, "Remember, the pilgrims were the ones who began this tradition when they had the first Thanksgiving dinner."

One by one, each person at the table named a special blessing—some big, some small—but each one very important to the grandparents, and especially important to God.

Gathered at the table that day was the son of the grandparents with his wife and children, the older daughter and her husband and children, and the younger daughter and her two sons.

How Aaron and Abigail enjoyed being right there in the dining room where they could hear the family talk and laugh together! The pilgrims were beginning to be very happy in their new home; they whispered to each other that indeed they had been brought to a wonderful place.

After Thanksgiving day passed, Aaron and Abigail still stood in front of the mirror on the special table in the dining room for several more days. All the grandchildren left except for two of the boys who spent many days at the grandparents' house. They played where Aaron and Abigail could watch them. One of the little boys especially liked to sit at the piano next to the table where the pilgrims stood; he would climb on top of a pillow on the bench and try to play songs. The other boy would sit at the table and draw wonderful pictures which the grandmother always put on display. The boys enjoyed playing hide and seek with the grandmother every chance they got. How the pilgrims liked to watch these two boys! The grandfather would come home for lunch, and the boys loved to sit and eat with him. Aaron and Abigail treasured their place right in the middle of all the fun the grandparents had with their two grandsons.

One day Aaron and Abigail heard wonderful music playing in the house. It reminded them of the music they used to hear in the store before they came to live in the grandparents' house. How they liked the sound of it! What the pilgrims didn't know was that it was Christmas music, and that meant it was time for a change of decorations.

To Aaron and Abigail's great surprise, the grandparents took away Ezra the Thanksgiving turkey, and the basket with all the fruits and vegetables and brightly colored leaves. Then the unthinkable happened! The grandparents came and took Aaron and Abigail and wrapped them in soft paper and placed them in the box from the store. The next thing they knew, they were on the shelves deep in the basement of the grandparents' house.

Now some folks might think that being placed on a shelf is a sad thing to do, and at first Aaron and Abigail thought so, too. They were sure that it was not going to be a happy place down in the basement. They felt lonely and forgotten. They heard the grandparents come down and take many decorations from the shelves. The grandparents gathered the decorations for the Christmas tree and the beautiful Christmas angel and then the Christmas village. Ezra told them that there were many empty spaces on the shelves now.

What Aaron and Abigail didn't know was that there was a special room that the grandfather had built for the grandchildren right near the shelves. It was a secret room under the stairs, not tall enough for an adult; only little people would fit into it. The boys would go in and pretend it was their own special house. What fun and laughter came from that room under the stairs! Sometimes there would be hammering and sawing noises as the boys pretended to build something with old pieces of wood. Sometimes it was just a wonderful place to hide when the older grandchildren came to play at the grandparents' house. It was always a happy place, this special room under the stairs.

What the two boys didn't know was that Aaron and

Abigail were listening to them play. They had no idea of the joy that they brought to the pilgrims when they came to play in the basement. Aaron and Abigail smiled when they heard the little boys laugh and felt sad when they cried.

The seasons came and went. The two boys came to visit the grandparents, sometimes staying for days at a time. Aaron and Abigail became quite used to being put back on the shelves when Thanksgiving passed and the Christmas season arrived. They knew the two boys would always come to the special basement room where they could hear them playing. How the pilgrims hoped that nothing would ever change; they liked everything just the way it was.

Slowly, however, things began to change. Aaron and Abigail thought they heard the boys' voices less and less. It seemed that the room under the stairs sat empty for weeks at a time. The boys came for visits, but they didn't stay as long as they used to, and the pilgrims missed them. Aaron and Abigail wondered what was wrong. Could it be the boys moved away, could it be the boys didn't enjoy being at the grandparents' house anymore? Aaron and Abigail were feeling sad and lonely for the first time since they had come to live at the grandparents' house.

The next time the pilgrims were put out on display, the grandparents noticed that they didn't have quite the same happy faces that they used to have. (Now it's important to remember that grandparents can hear and see things that other people can't.) So the grandparents sat down near Aaron and Abigail and asked them why they looked so unhappy. The pilgrims said they really missed the two boys who used to spend so much time at the grandparents' house. They didn't hear them playing in the room under the stairs or see them running past the table where the pilgrims stood in front of the mirror. They wanted to know what had happened to the two boys.

The grandparents explained to Aaron and Abigail that the two boys were older now, and they had to go to school. Their life had changed and they were very busy and happy but had less time to spend at the grandparents' house. The grandparents explained that the boys still loved them as much as always even though they didn't come to visit as often.

Aaron and Abigail learned an important lesson that day. They learned that even though things had changed all around them, they were still pilgrims with a purpose. They had a special job that no one else could do for the grandparents. Only they could stand there in front of the mirror in the dining room and remind everyone of the very first Thanksgiving. They had been especially chosen by the grandparents for that purpose.

Real people need to learn that no matter how much life may change all around them God has a special purpose for each one. When the time is right, God will put them to use in that special place that only they can fill.

Chapter Five

SAMSON AND NOAH, THE GUARD DOGS

Long, long ago when the grandmother was just a little girl, the amazing adventures of Samson and Noah began. Noah and Samson were guard dogs; not the kind of guard dogs that one would normally think of. They were very special guard dogs. Their job was to guard the heart of a precious little girl, and on Valentine's Day, the grandmother always remembers their story.

Noah and Samson were lovely little dogs made of ceramic. Samson was the larger of the two. They both had brown spots and little coal black eyes. At the beginning of our story they don't live on the shelves deep in the basement of the grandparents' house with Amos the Pumpkin, or Aaron and Abigail the Pilgrims, and they had not yet met Obadiah the Christmas Star, but one day they would!

Samson and Noah originally belonged to the mother of the little girl in our story. The mother became very sick one day. She knew that she would soon leave her little girl and go to heaven. She slipped the little dogs into her daughter's pocket and asked them to guard her heart. The mother knew the little girl would be very sad in the days to come, and she wanted Samson and Noah to help her.

The day soon came when Samson and Noah had their first big job. The little girl was at her mom's grave, clutching a single red rose. Samson and Noah could almost hear her little heart breaking. It was time for them to do all they could to guard her heart, so they snuggled as close to her as they could. They tried to let her know they were there, and that she would be all right.

As the little girl slipped her hand into her pocket and felt the little dogs, she knew they were trying very hard to comfort her. She remembered her mom had put them there, and through them she could almost feel the love her mom had for her.

Soon the little girl would begin a journey to a place she had never been, and she would be going there with people she hardly knew. She would have to leave behind all that was familiar to her.

The next day the little girl was in a new apartment, sitting at the breakfast table and looking out the window. Since the apartment was on the second floor, she could look down on her new neighborhood. The lady who was to care for the little girl over the coming years served her oatmeal, and oh, how the little girl detested oatmeal! She thought about the peanut butter bread that her mom used to serve her. The little girl felt very alone and frightened, and her heart began to break. Once more she remembered the little guard dogs, Samson and Noah, who were right inside her pocket. She could feel them snuggling as close as they possibly could, and she felt brave once more.

During the days, weeks, months, and years that followed, the little girl would have a great need for her little friends, Samson and Noah. Some days she would swing on the porch of the upstairs apartment and wonder about her mom who had gone to live in heaven with Jesus. What did that really mean? Was there really a heaven and would she ever see her mother again?

She missed the farm where she used to live before her mom died. She was sad, lonely, and brokenhearted, but she would always remember Samson and Noah nestled deep within her pocket. She could almost hear them say, "Don't be afraid, it will be all right, be brave!"

She would always feel better when she remembered the little guard dogs.

The years went by…the little girl grew…the people she lived with moved to a different town. She had to get used to a new neighborhood and school, and lots of new people. The day came when the little girl had to walk to school in the new town, all by herself. She was frightened because she wasn't sure she could find her way all alone. Sure enough, she got lost, or at least she felt lost. She stood on the sidewalk, very frightened, feeling very alone. As she remembered her little guard dogs inside her pocket, she slipped her hand in and felt Samson and Noah, and she could almost hear them saying, "Don't be afraid, it will be all right." Sure enough, she found her way to school, and her heart felt brave again.

The girl loved to sit at the window in her upstairs bedroom and daydream about the future. She was often very lonely and missed everything she had left behind when her mother died. The girl would look out her window and pretend that she could look into the future and imagined a life filled with joy and happiness.

The young girl became a teenager in high school and made friends with some of her classmates. Sometimes she had so much fun with them she almost forgot her unhappiness. The girl now had more freedom to come and go on her own, and with this freedom came opportunities, some good and some that were not good. She was sometimes tempted to do some of the forbidden things that she saw other people her age doing. It always seemed that just as she was about to get into trouble, she would remember Samson and Noah, still nestled in her pocket. She could almost hear them saying, "We are here to guard your heart, please do the right thing." The girl was so grateful that her little friends were always there to encourage her in times of weakness.

Time passed and the girl grew into a young woman. She was old enough to take care of herself and begin the life she had been dreaming of for so many years. What would she do? Now that she was ready to be on her own, she realized that she had many choices about her future. It was an exciting, yet scary time, but she was always comforted by the knowledge that whatever she decided to do, Samson and Noah would be close by to encourage her.

One day the young woman met a very handsome young man, and they became friends. She met his family and found, to her delight, that this was the kind of family she had always dreamed of having. They had such fun together and loved each other the way she always thought families should love each other. How she enjoyed the time she spent with this family!

One glorious day the young man and the young woman were married. She was happier than she had been since she was a little girl. Her heart had not felt so full of joy in such a long time. They moved into a little house, and their home was filled with love and happiness. Samson and Noah were very happy, too, but they wondered if the young woman still needed them or if their job was completed.

The years passed, and three children were added to the family—two girls and a boy. The young woman, who was now the mother, wanted more than anything to make their home a place where her children would be happy, where they would never be afraid, lonely, or sad. Samson and Noah stayed close to the girl who had become a woman and was now the mother. They found her heart was hardly ever sad and she needed them less and less. They had to admit they missed being needed.

As the children grew, the mother came to understand that she was not strong enough or wise enough to make sure her children were always happy. This was a great concern to the young mother. She wondered if Samson and Noah could help her children the way they had helped her, but she soon realized that the children didn't see or hear the little dogs in the same way she always had. She spent many hours worrying about the happiness that she wanted for her children.

One day someone told the young mother that only God could guard her children the way she wanted them guarded. He was able to watch over her children far better than even she or her husband could. She learned that God loved her children more than even she did.

As the young mother learned more and more about the love that God had for her children, she learned that He loved her and watched over her all those years when she was a frightened little girl. She came to understand that when she heard Samson and Noah telling her to be brave, it was really the voice of God giving her courage and strength. She now knew that she had never really been alone at all. God had been there with her all the time. He had used Samson and Noah as a sign of His care and concern.

Samson and Noah remained very important to the girl who was now a grandmother. They now make their home deep in the basement of the grandparents' house. They live on the shelves with all the special decorations, Amos the Pumpkin, Aaron and Abigail the pilgrims, and Obadiah the Christmas star.

Samson and Noah come out at Christmas time and are part of the Christmas village. They have a special place of honor at the train station in the village, where they sit and watch for the grandchildren to come and visit.

This year, however, they are going to have a place of honor all through February in honor of Valentine's day, because the little girl, who is now all grown up and a grandmother, wants to remember how God used them to help guard her heart.

Chapter Six

OBADIAH, THE CHRISTMAS STAR

Long ago, before the grandparents were grandparents, there were children who lived in the house. They weren't grandchildren—they were just children, and the grandparents were their parents.

It was getting close to Christmas. How the children looked forward to Christmas and all the decorations! It was a very special time of year indeed. They loved to decorate the tree with all the ornaments, each one special because of who made it or a memory that the ornament held. The mother put out the nativity scene with Mary, Joseph, and the baby Jesus, and the family put lights in each of the windows. When they were finished, everyone piled into the car, and they drove all around town to look at how all the other houses were decorated for Christmas. What fun it was to see all the colorful, bright lights! Sometimes they even baked a birthday cake for Jesus and sang "Happy Birthday" to Him since they were celebrating His birthday.

One day at the beginning of the Christmas season, the father said to the boy, "I think something is missing at our house." The father had a wonderful idea and took the boy out to the workshop where they spent the afternoon sawing wood and hammering nails. When they had finished, they had created a big Christmas star. The father got some lights and put them on the star. Then he climbed a ladder and put the star up on the house and plugged it in. It was the most beautiful Christmas star the boy had ever seen!

Each year the family decorated the house with the tree, lights, shiny garlands, and the nativity set. Then the biggest decoration of all went up—Obadiah the Christmas star was lifted high onto the roof and plugged in. The father, the mother, and all the children would stand back and admire Obadiah. He reminded them of the star that led the wise men to Jesus many long years ago. Obadiah was very happy; he liked to remind people of the One whom Christmas was really all about.

The years went by…each year Obadiah looked forward to the time when the father and the son would come and get him and put him in that special place on the roof of the house where he welcomed people who came to visit. Obadiah knew that the family looked forward to seeing him each year as much as he looked forward to seeing them.

Obadiah stood proudly on the roof of the house. He especially liked it when snowflakes would drop gently onto him. The layers of snow on Obadiah made him glow all the more. When his lights shown out through the whiteness, Obadiah sparkled like hundreds of tiny jewels, and he winked at all the families who drove by to look at him. The children who lived in the house always enjoyed seeing Obadiah shining each time they came home. They even tried to see if they could spot Obadiah from the end of the road. The joy he brought to the family made him a very happy star!

After the Christmas season passed, he lived deep down in the basement with Aaron & Abigail, the pilgrims, Amos the pumpkin, the Easter decorations and, of course, all the Christmas ornaments. Since Obadiah was much too big to live on the shelves like the other decorations, he just leaned against the shelves. As long as he was near the others, he was quite content.

As each holiday came, the decorations were taken

upstairs to the main part of the house where they were carefully and lovingly put out to make the holiday extra special. Then, when the holiday was over, the decorations were brought back to the shelves where they would tell the others about all the wonderful sights they had seen as they sat in their place of honor. Year after year, Obadiah so enjoyed the time when he and the other Christmas decorations were brought out. He was a very happy Christmas star indeed.

Obadiah hoped life would always stay the same. Little did he know that big changes would one day come! The children were getting older, but it happened so slowly that no one really noticed, least of all Obadiah. He would watch the children play while he leaned against the shelves.

One by one the children who lived in the house spent less and less time playing in the basement. Obadiah noticed that he almost never saw the girls who lived in the house anymore. Sometimes he could hear them talking with their friends, and occasionally they would pass by the shelves to get something from the storage room, but they usually rushed off.

For a long time, Obadiah was happy because the boy who helped build him played in the basement near the storage shelves. He and his friends would sometimes build and paint and do what boys like to do.

Each year when the Christmas decorations were put out to make the house beautiful for the holiday, new decorations were added. Obadiah especially liked the little Christmas village with people singing carols and children skating on a pond. It seemed that the shelf which held the Christmas decorations was growing more and more crowded as the years went by.

Then one Christmas, the father came alone to get Obadiah and the other Christmas decorations, and only the mother stood and watched as Obadiah was plugged in. Obadiah still sparkled and winked as he had other years, but something was different. The house was still brightly decorated; guests still came to visit; but it was not as it had been in years before. The children, who now seemed so much bigger, were only there for a little while and then they were gone again!

After Christmas passed, the parents took the decorations down, just as they did every year. They packed them gently away and put them back on the shelves deep in the basement. Obadiah was always the last decoration to come down. The family always felt a little sad when it was time to take him down and put him away for another year.

This year, however, something happened to Obadiah that he never expected. The father took Obadiah down as usual, but instead of carrying him to the basement and leaning him against the shelves, the father carried him out to the garage. The father climbed a ladder, put Obadiah up in the wooden beams supporting the garage, climbed down, shut the garage door, and went away leaving Obadiah all alone.

Obadiah was shocked! *Why was I put out here in the*

garage? What could I have done to deserve this? he wondered. He was very sad and lonely and cold. He had never felt cold when he stood on the roof of the house; even when the snow gently fell on him he always felt warm and happy and cozy.

Obadiah felt that his world had ended. First the children whom he loved so much had disappeared, and now he no longer lived down in the basement with the other decorations. He was sad, and he was very lonely.

Obadiah saw the father and mother come and go when they parked their cars in the garage. Sometimes the father looked up at Obadiah, but mostly they didn't even seem to notice that he was there. Obadiah looked down at them and wished they would say hello, but they never did. That Spring when the garage door was left open, he could see visitors coming and going, but they never noticed that there was a very lonely Christmas star living out there.

Slowly Obadiah began to adjust to his new home. Now that he lived out in the garage, he started to enjoy the Summer almost as much as he did the Winter. The garage door was almost always left open during the day, and he could hear birds singing and sometimes see people walking by the house. He could hear the mother and father and their friends having picnics and parties on the deck nearby; but best of all, he sometimes saw the boy and his sisters when they came to visit the parents. They were much older now, and it seemed that they had forgotten all about Obadiah, but Obadiah had not forgotten about them. He remembered all the happy days when the boy and his sisters lived in the house and played in the basement by the shelves.

Then, once again there was a chill in the air, and the ground was white with frost in the morning. Obadiah knew that Christmas was coming soon. The father came out to the garage, climbed up the ladder, and got Obadiah down. He took him out and put him in his place of honor on the roof of the house where the snow began to gently fall on him. He sparkled like a hundred tiny jewels, and he winked at people as they drove by. How happy he was to be back out where he could see the other decorations through the windows! He had missed them so much.

One year on a bright December day as Obadiah stood guard on the roof of the house, a car came slowly up the road. He could see a little boy and girl in the car with their noses pressed against the window, and they were looking up at him. The car stopped at the house; out climbed a father, a mother, and the boy and girl. They walked over to look up at Obadiah. As they stood there, Obadiah suddenly realized that this father was the boy who had helped to build him many years ago. He was all grown up and now was a father himself. The man told his family how he and his father had built the beautiful Christmas star so long ago.

The children looked up at Obadiah and smiled in a way he hadn't remembered since the children had done when they were little boys and girls. He was once again a truly happy Christmas star. Now Obadiah didn't mind it when he went back to live in the garage after Christmas was over.

Soon there were many grandchildren. When they came to the grandparents' house to visit, they often played outside, rode bicycles, and drew pictures on the driveway with chalk. From his home in the rafters, he could watch it all.

Obadiah learned a very important lesson: he learned that when scary changes came into his life, he could trust the grandparents. Something new and wonderful can be found in the most unexpected places.

Chapter Seven

MICAH, THE PERFECT CHRISTMAS TREE

Micah began his life as a small seedling in a very large forest. He was surrounded by many other trees, most of which were much larger than him. For many years, Micah couldn't see anything but darkness. He was so small that the other trees blocked the sunlight, and if you walked through the forest you might accidentally step on him and not even notice. Fortunately for little Micah, no one walked in that particular part of the forest then, so no one stepped on him.

Little by little Micah grew taller and stronger. He began to enjoy the wonderful warmth that covered his branches. Since he could now see more than just the floor of the forest, he was surprised to discover a whole world of nature around him. He could see the warmth he felt on his branches came from the bright sunlight streaming down from the sky. Micah felt sure it had been partly responsible for the growth that had taken place in his trunk and branches.

When the bright sun disappeared at night and darkness surrounded him, he noticed there were lovely little lights sparkling in the sky above him. Micah always enjoyed those times. The taller he grew, the closer he felt to the twinkling lights. Micah especially loved it when snow fell from the sky and landed on him and all the other trees nearby. When the sun rose high in the sky, it would melt the snow and make him feel all new and clean.

As time went by, Micah noticed that his place in the forest was becoming more and more crowded. It seemed that his branches were finding it harder and harder to stretch out. Micah was pleased with how he had grown and wished he had more room to display his splendid greenery.

One day, to Micah's great surprise, his desire for more room became a reality. Some people came into his part of the forest with things that Micah had never seen before. One person had an ax, and another had a saw. Micah couldn't believe it, but each of them began to cut down the trees around him. When they were finished, Micah had much more room to stretch out his branches, and the warmth from the sun shone more brightly than he had ever seen it. But Micah became very sad when he watched the people drag the cut trees out of the forest. Micah wondered where they were being taken and what would happen to them.

As the years went by, Micah stood ever taller in the forest. He loved to watch the animals as they ran and played around him. Sometimes the squirrels would climb up his trunk, and the birds would land in his branches, but his favorite visitor was a lovely deer with gentle eyes. When the snow got deep, and it was too difficult for her to travel through the forest, she would come and make a bed under Micah's branches and wait for the storm to pass.

Micah learned to tell when a change of seasons was about to happen. He saw some of the trees around him become clothed in yellow, orange, and red leaves. Then they would lose them just as he lost some of his old pine needles in the gusts of wind that always came that time of year. He knew that soon the snow would fall and cover them all.

Micah was always very excited when the days grew

longer once again, and the sun shone brighter, and he could see the colorful wildflowers growing on the ground all around him. Everything seemed new and bright and fresh during this season. Leaves were sprouting on the branches of the trees that were bare, and he would have lots of new needles and pinecones on his.

Then came the days when the sun got stronger and it felt so much hotter. The whole forest looked forward to the afternoon rains that would cool them down.

Soon the time came when the nights were chilly and the leaves on the trees in the forest began to change color once again. Micah noticed a pattern to the changes—each change brought new things to enjoy. He was one happy evergreen tree…most of the time.

Everything seemed perfect to Micah—except for those times when people came into the forest. He worried because some of the trees around him were cut down and dragged out of the forest. He was afraid the same thing would happen to him.

One bright snowy day, a group of people came into the forest where Micah stood. There were two adults and two children. He heard their laughter and singing; he liked the sounds very much and was surprised because he had never heard any of the other people sound so happy. They spent a great deal of time looking over Micah and all the other evergreen trees in the forest. He wondered what they were doing and why they were inspecting the trees so carefully.

The little girl asked her father to tell her the story of Christmas and why a Christmas tree was so important. When Micah heard the words, “Christmas tree,” his branches really perked up; he wanted to hear this story, too!

The father began to tell the story of how long ago God had sent a baby, His own dear Son, to earth to be the Savior of the world. The man said this baby’s name was Jesus. Micah was amazed to hear that people had done bad things and needed to be forgiven. The man went on to tell how Jesus grew up and became a man and gave His life so that people could live forever with Him in heaven.

The father explained that trees were a very important part of Christmas. He said that because the evergreen tree stays green all year it reminds them of the everlasting life that God gives to those who believe in Him. He went on to say that the majestic branches of a tree seem to be reaching up to heaven, reaching toward God, and when lights are put on the tree they sparkle like the stars. He said they remind them that Jesus is the light of the world.

Soon the family found just the tree they were looking for, and the father began to cut it down. When he had finished, they dragged the tree to their car, singing Christmas carols all the way. For the first time, Micah was sad to see people leave.

Micah couldn’t stop thinking about the story that the man had told. He was very excited to know that there was a loving God, and surely this God was his Creator as well. He was certain that God had created him for the special purpose of being a Christmas tree. He now understood why he loved the warm sun on his branches and why he loved to see the stars in the sky overhead. He knew they were put there by this loving God.

Now he looked forward to people coming into the forest; he knew it was Christmas time and they were looking for a tree to take home. He no longer worried about being cut down by a saw or an ax and dragged from the forest. In fact, he longed for the day when someone would come along and choose him to be their Christmas tree. Each time people came into the forest he tried to stand as straight and tall as he possibly could, hoping that it was his turn to be chosen as a very special Christmas tree. Although he knew that he would eventually die since he was no longer attached to his roots, he didn't mind at all. He knew this was the purpose he was created for, and that was enough for him.

The special day that Micah had waited for finally arrived! A family came into the forest and looked over all the trees. Then the grandmother saw Micah and went straight over to him. She walked around him; she felt his needles and inspected his trunk to make sure it was nice and straight; she sniffed his branches; and at last shouted to the rest of her family, "I have found the perfect tree for our home, come and see!" The rest of the family ran over to her, and each one declared Micah to be "the perfect tree." Micah knew that at last he was going to have his chance!

The grandfather cut Micah down, and he and the grandchildren all worked hard to carry him from the forest. They carefully loaded Micah into the trunk, and the next thing he knew he was in the home of the grandparents. All the wonderful decorations were taken from the shelves deep in the basement of the grandparents' house and lovingly placed on Micah. The grandchildren, the children, and the grandparents all talked about how special each decoration was, where it had come from, and all the memories attached to it. And everyone that came to visit said that they had indeed found the perfect Christmas tree.

Micah didn't mind at all that he was no longer in the forest under the sparkling stars in the sky. Now he was covered with beautiful twinkling lights and people were all around him singing about the Savior he had first heard of years before.

He especially liked it at night when all the people went to bed and the house was quiet. That was when all the decorations talked to each other about everything that happened in the grandparents' house. Micah was a very happy tree, and he knew that he had fulfilled his special purpose in life.

Chapter Eight

HOSEA, THE HIDING PLACE

Long ago when the grandfather was just a boy, he loved to build things with his father, who was a carpenter. Over the years, he built many toys and even a tree house. One special thing that he created has lived at the grandparents' home ever since they were first married.

The grandfather created Hosea to be a rack that can be hung on a wall. Now Hosea isn't a particularly beautiful creation, but he is a very useful one. He even has a secret compartment with a door that can be locked.

For a long time, he was hung on a wall for everyone to see. Hosea always liked that best because then he could be useful. But Hosea was not always needed. During those times, he was shoved into the back of a closet where no one saw him. For awhile, Hosea was even put into storage deep in the basement, near the shelves where the decorations and ornaments lived. Hosea didn't really mind it because he liked being around lots of activity.

The years went by and children were born to the parents. The sounds of the children's laughter filling the house were wonderful to hear. From his place near the shelves, Hosea watched the children as they happily played downstairs.

Hosea could always tell what time of year it was because he saw the family come and gather the decorations that were needed for the special holidays. Hosea watched Amos and the other Fall and harvest decorations leave and return. Then Aaron and Abigail and all the Thanksgiving decorations would have their turn. And finally, Christmas would come and Obadiah and all the other beautiful decorations would be taken up to decorate the house for the holiday.

Hosea was not one to complain, but he often felt a little sad when he saw all the decorations and ornaments come and go. He was grateful that at least he was in the house and the father had always taken him along each time they moved.

One day Hosea heard loud noises coming from upstairs in the house. There was lots of pounding, hammering, sawing, and all sorts of activity. Hosea and all the decorations and ornaments had never heard such a racket! It went on day after day after day. Then suddenly it stopped, and everything was quiet again.

It wasn't long after the noise stopped that the father came downstairs to get Hosea. To Hosea's great delight, the father carried him upstairs and into what looked like a brand new beautiful room. Then the most wonderful thing happened—the father hung Hosea on the wall of the little boy's room!

Finally, he was in a place where he could do exactly what he was created to do many years before. The boy hung his fishing rod and his baseball glove and cap on him. Then the boy unlocked the secret compartment and put special things inside. It was so wonderful!

Hosea especially enjoyed it when the mother or father would come upstairs to tuck the boy into bed at night. The boy told his parents about his day, and they prayed with him and kissed him goodnight.

Sometimes the boy's two sisters would come into the room—that was always lots of fun. Some nights he could hear the sisters across the hall laughing and talking. Hosea had never heard anything like the giggling that went on when the girls had friends come for a sleepover in their room. Life was good for Hosea; there was always something for him to watch while he hung on the wall in the boy's bedroom.

Over the years, the boy grew and so did his sisters. The things that the boy hung on Hosea changed, and so did the things that he locked in the secret compartment. The fishing rods and the baseball gloves got larger and larger.

The boy began to spend less time in his bedroom. Hosea didn't hear much noise from the sisters' room across the hall either. The older sister had gone off to college, and before long the younger one went, too. Then one day the boy, who had now became a man, left the room for good. He packed his clothes and took all of his fishing rods and his baseball glove. He even unlocked the secret compartment and took all the things that were there. Hosea had a very strange feeling that things weren't going to be the same again.

Well, Hosea was right. Things were never quite the same again. The upstairs of the grandparents' house became quiet and dark and very lonely. Hosea's arms which once held the fishing rods and his secret compartment were empty.

Over the years, there were sometimes guests who slept in the room where Hosea lived, but they hardly ever noticed him and almost never hung anything on his arms—and they never, ever, put anything in his secret compartment.

It wasn't long before more changes came to the

rooms upstairs in the grandparents' house.The furniture changed—a crib was set up. Soon there was the sound of a crying baby, and then there was another baby, and then yet another. The two sisters and the boy were now all grown up and they came back to the grandparents' house to visit, bringing their babies with them. The upstairs was filled with noise and laughter once again. Hosea loved it when the grandchildren came upstairs to take their naps. He didn't even mind when they cried; he was just happy not to be alone.

As time went on, the number of grandchildren grew—there were lots of them, some boys and some girls. What fun they were to watch! At first the grandchildren didn't pay any attention to Hosea. They were still too small to hang things on his arms, and they couldn't possibly reach his secret compartment; but he didn't mind, he was just happy when they were around.

The years passed and the grandchildren began to visit the grandparents' house without their parents for several days. When that happened, there was lots of excitement. The grandchildren would spend hours upstairs playing games like hide and seek and talking about all the fun things that grandchildren love to share with each other.

As the grandchildren grew, they began to notice Hosea for the first time. They looked him over, and one of them noticed that he had a secret compartment with a lock. Now, of course, this was of great interest to the grandchildren because children love secret compartments. They found the key and unlocked it, expecting to find some wonderful treasure. They were quite disappointed when they found it empty.

One of the grandchildren came up with the idea of hiding some of their treasures in Hosea's secret compartment. The rest of them got very excited and hunted up some of the things they had brought with them. They put them inside and locked the door. Then they hid the key in a dresser drawer so any of them could open it whenever they came for a visit.

Hosea was so excited that he could hardly stand it. He still didn't have much hanging on his arms—just a couple of old hats—but oh, his secret compartment was always full! Now every time one of the grandchildren came to visit, the first thing they did was run upstairs, get the key from its hiding place, unlock the secret compartment, and see what was left inside by whoever had last visited the grandparents' house. Hosea was happier than he ever remembered being in his whole life.

How Hosea's life had changed over the years! He had sometimes been on display; he had sometimes been in storage; but Hosea had never been forgotten by his creator. Real people need to remember that their Creator made them for a special purpose just as Hosea's creator had made him. And just like Hosea, real people can be sure that their Creator will always take very good care of them.

Chapter Nine

ELIJAH, THE GREAT BOOMER

Summertime was not a favorite time of the year for most of the decorations and ornaments who lived on the shelves deep in the basement of the grandparent's house. It got very hot and humid down there then, and most of the children's play went on outside so that the house seemed pretty empty.

Before there were grandchildren, when there were only children who lived at the grandparents' house, they loved the warm Summer days when they could play outside all day long. The mother packed them picnic lunches, and they climbed the hill behind their house and sat in the shade of a giant willow tree. They ate peanut butter and jelly sandwiches and drank delicious cold lemonade and talked about the adventures they would have in the afternoon.

A row of big old trees lined the backyard where the children made a little playhouse. They spent many happy hours there. Sometimes they had tea parties (though the little boy thought they were a little silly); other times they played hide and seek among the trees. To the children, the playhouse seemed like a beautiful castle.

On many of those hot, humid days, the mother put a small tub of water out on the lawn so the children could cool off. They enjoyed that special treat—they pretended they had a lake all to themselves. Once in a while, the mother gave the children a garden hose, and they gleefully sprayed each other and ran through the stream of water for hours at a time.

Each day brought new adventures and games to play. Sometimes they would lie on the soft, green grass and watch interesting shapes form in the big puffy clouds overhead.

The children especially loved to play outside after dark on warm, Summer nights. They caught fireflies and put them in glass jars. They enjoyed watching the lights glow on and off as the fireflies flew around inside the jar. The mother always had the children set the fireflies free before they came inside to get ready for bed.

Occasionally there would be rainy days, and the children would be forced to play inside. The decorations and ornaments loved rainy days, for that meant they could enjoy watching and listening to the children as they played downstairs. Rainy days went by oh so slowly for the children, but they went by all too quickly for the decorations on the shelves.

Elijah was one resident of the shelves deep in the basement of the grandparents' house who just loved the Summer. He was very happy when the days grew longer and it got hot, humid, and sticky down in the basement. He would tingle with excitement because it meant his special day was coming.

Nobody remembered just how old Elijah was, but he had been around for a long, long time. He was a special gift from an old friend of the grandparents. Elijah was just the right name for him, too. Like the prophet with the same name in the Bible, when Elijah spoke, everybody listened! He didn't speak often, but when he did it was always exciting.

The Fourth of July was a very important holiday to the grandparents, especially the grandfather. He loved to celebrate America's birthday, and he always planned a big birthday party. When the family returned from watching the annual parade, the party would begin. Elijah's job was to add fun and loud excitement, and he never failed to do just that.

Now Elijah wasn't much to look at. Some said he kind of looked like a shiny tin can. But Elijah was designed so that with the grandfather's help he could send a ball flying high into the sky. But that wasn't all he could do. When the ball flew from Elijah's mouth he made the biggest boom you have ever heard. Everyone knew that the loud boom was really Elijah saying "Happy Birthday, America!"

When he sent the ball climbing high into the sky, everyone looked at him with respect, and they all cheered the wonderful job he did. The children watched to see where the ball landed. They raced to be the first to find it and bring it back to Elijah and the grandfather. Then they excitedly waited for Elijah to make the ball once again climb high into the sky.

This wonderful game went on for much of the Fourth of July. Guests who came to celebrate with the family joined in the fun of finding the ball. Sometimes it seemed that Elijah would run out of steam and had to take a short rest, but before long he was ready to go, and the game would start all over again.

Elijah's only problem was that, unlike the other decorations and ornaments on the shelves deep in the basement of the grandparents house, his special day was just that—only one day each year. The other decorations were put on display for days or even weeks before an actual holiday. But for Elijah that was not the case. Once his day had passed, he was put away until the next year. As you can imagine, Elijah was very sad when his special day was over.

Elijah always knew when it was about to come to an end. He heard the sounds of explosions far away and could see the glare of bright lights high in the sky. Elijah understood that this could only mean one thing—the fireworks display was beginning. While everyone else watched the fireworks, poor Elijah knew his work was done, and he would be put away for another year.

Elijah tried to be very brave and not get angry when he was put back on the shelves. He tried very hard to be thankful for the one day he did have with the family and their guests, so he worked to do his job the very best he could.

As the years went by, Elijah grew rather old and rusty looking. He lost most of his paint, and he wasn't nearly as shiny as he was when he was first created. But since it wasn't his looks that made him important, the grandparents never did much to clean him up.

In the meantime, the children became all grown up. They moved away from the grandparents' house, but they always came back to celebrate the birthday of America each year. And each year it seemed that when they came back, they brought more children with them—children who begged the grandfather to get old Elijah and fire him up, sending the ball climbing into the sky! They loved to see who would be the first one to find the ball and bring it back to Elijah and the grandfather so they could do it all over again.

It seemed that the grandfather never got tired of helping Elijah hurl the ball into the sky. Elijah had to rest more often than he used to—after all he was getting old—but oh how he loved to hear the grandchildren squeal with delight when the ball shot into the sky and Elijah boomed out, "Happy Birthday, America!"

One particular year on the fifth of July, Elijah was feeling especially sad…well, really angry about his situation. He looked at himself—*What a mess*, he thought. He was scratched, dented, and he had completely lost his shine. He realized the other decorations, all of whom were as old as him, still looked fresh and clean. He wondered why they were so much better cared for than he was. He was not a happy resident on the shelves deep in the basement of the grandparents' house. Why wasn't he treated the same way as all the other residents on the shelves? *What is wrong with me?* he wondered. Elijah spent a long, miserable year thinking about his situation.

Finally the Fourth of July came again. All the grandchildren and their parents arrived as soon as the parade was over, and as always, the grandchildren's first request to the grandfather was "Let's have Elijah!" The party was never officially under way until Elijah was there sending the ball climbing into the sky and shouting "Happy Birthday, America!"

The grandfather got old Elijah from the basement. The grandchildren lined up with great anticipation and held their breath while waiting to see the ball hurled into the sky and hear the big boom. But to everyone's surprise, the ball did not climb into the sky; it barely made out of Elijah's mouth and plopped silently on the ground at the grandfather's feet. Everyone stood in stunned silence. What could be wrong with poor old Elijah? The grandfather quickly took him into his workshop to see if he could find out what had happened to old Elijah and see if he could be repaired.

(Now it is important to remember that grandparents can hear things no one else can hear.) The grandfather asked Elijah what the problem was. Elijah told the grandfather he wanted to be given a new holiday to celebrate. He was unhappy to be brought outside for only one day of the year. He wanted a new job. He was not going to send the ball flying into the air, and he surely would never again shout "Happy Birthday, America!" Elijah told the grandfather to let one of the other decorations do his job from now on.

The grandfather grew very sad. He told Elijah if he didn't send the ball flying high into the sky, the children would never again be able to race to find it when it fell to the ground. And if Elijah wouldn't shout "Happy Birthday, America!" then no one would ever hear that happy sound again.

The grandfather explained to Elijah that no one else could do his job because no one else had been created in the same way he was. He had just the right equipment to hurl the ball high into the sky and make that wonderful booming shout about America's birthday. The grandfather told him he was one of a kind, and no one could ever replace him. It was not what Elijah looked like that made him so important, it was what was on the inside that made him the only one who could make the Fourth of July a wonderful and exciting holiday for everyone.

Elijah thought for a moment as he lay on the bench in the grandfather's workshop. He finally understood who he was and why he was created. He realized he made a very big mistake by comparing himself to the other decorations and ornaments. They had a special job, but so did he. He began to feel very ashamed of himself. He thought to himself, *If only the grandfather will give me another chance, I will send that ball higher than ever before, and I will shout "Happy Birthday, America!" louder than ever before. I will be grateful for who and what I am.*

Well, the grandfather did give Elijah another chance. He quickly shined old Elijah up and brought him outside. He put the ball into his mouth and set him off. Sure enough, the ball went higher and farther than it had ever gone before, and Elijah shouted "Happy Birthday, America!" so loudly the neighbors came out to see what all the noise was about. It took the grandchildren a very long time to find the ball, but find it they did. Time after time that day Elijah happily did his job better than he had ever done it before.

When the fireworks began and the fireflies came out, Elijah felt a little sad because he knew soon he would go back to the shelves for another year. This time, however, he went with a thankful heart that he was one of a kind with a very special job to do.

Sometimes real people forget how very special they are. They forget that God has made them unique and that they shouldn't compare themselves to other people because they can never be replaced by anyone else.

Chapter Ten

PHOEBE, THE BUNNY OF HOPE

Spring was a favorite time of year for the grandparents. Long before the grandparents ever thought of being grandparents, or even parents for that matter, they were married in the Spring when they were very young.

At this time of year, the new blades of green grass

spring up and the first little faces of the purple crocus and yellow daffodils lift their heads up toward the sun. Soon everything that looked dead and gray begins to come to life again. The trees burst forth with fresh new leaves. The earth is covered with a more lovely shade of green in the Spring than at any other time of the year. The wonderful thing about this season is no matter how long the Winter has been, or how dark and dreary the landscape looks, Spring always comes, every single year without fail.

The first year after the grandparents were married was a wonderful year, and they thought they could not possibly be any happier. They thought Spring was more glorious that year than ever before.

The next Spring, the first of the children was born to the parents, who were now even happier. A beautiful baby girl was born on the Sunday before Easter. Along with the arrival of this beautiful child came an Easter bunny, and this bunny's name was Phoebe. No one can remember exactly where Phoebe came from, she was just always there. Phoebe spent her time lying in the bed with the baby girl, watching over her as she slept.

When the next Spring arrived, they celebrated their little girl's first birthday. The parents decided to also celebrate Easter. They gave Phoebe a special place among the Easter decorations. After all, Phoebe was a very special bunny. The parents colored eggs and gave the little girl a tiny taste of her first chocolate Easter bunny.

Another year passed and to the great delight of the

parents, another little girl was added to their family. It seemed that each Spring and Easter brought with it something new and exciting. Phoebe the bunny loved Spring, and especially Easter, because it seemed then she was treated with much greater importance than at any other time of the year. Now that there were two little girls, the parents had even more fun at Easter. They filled baskets for the girls with colored eggs, chocolate eggs and bunnies, and lots of brightly colored jelly beans.

A few years later, another child was added to the family. Now this baby was not a little girl, and this baby was not born in the Spring. The little girls were very excited to have a little brother and loved him very much, and so did Phoebe.

As the years passed, the Easter celebrations became more and more fun. The children would hop out of bed in the morning and run downstairs to see what delicious goodies might be left in their Easter baskets. Phoebe was always sitting beside the baskets on Easter morning. The children thought that Phoebe had somehow filled those baskets, so Phoebe loved this part of Easter most of all!

After inspecting their baskets, the children could hardly wait to begin the Easter egg hunt. Once in awhile, Easter came when there was still snow on the ground. Then the hunt would take place down in the basement, near the shelves where all the decorations lived (much to their delight). The parents hid brightly colored eggs in all sorts of places. Each child searched high and low to see who could find the most colored eggs.

If the weather was warm enough, the eggs were hidden outside under shrubs and behind trees and in the grass. The children scattered across the yard looking for eggs, each one hoping to be the one who found the most. Sometimes the children took part in a community Easter egg hunt where there were many children all running in different directions looking for eggs in a big field; but most of all, the children loved the Easter egg hunts at home with the parents and with Phoebe.

Phoebe was grateful she could stay with the family through all the seasons of the year. She was allowed to be with the family all year long since she had arrived at the same time as the first baby girl.

During the long Winters, the days were crisp and cold and the children spent their time outside sledding and building snowmen and snow forts. It was all great fun for the whole family. The days always ended with cups of steaming hot chocolate. Soon the tired children were tucked into bed, and Phoebe was always close by to watch over them through the night.

When the Winters passed, the days began to grow just a bit longer. The snow took on the color of dull gray and began to melt, leaving piles of sand in its place. The parents began to think about Spring and the wonder of how the earth went from drab and dead to alive with color and beauty. It seemed like a miracle to the parents that the earth came alive every single year, without fail.

This year they had long talks about Spring and the beauty that it brought. The mother could not sleep at night for thinking about Springtime and its faithful return. She had a feeling that there was much more to Easter than brightly colored eggs, Easter egg hunts, and chocolate bunnies.

Phoebe heard them talking and got very worried. She thought that she was surely the most important part of Easter. After all, hadn't she come to live with the parents and the first little girl in the Spring, and hadn't she watched over the children all their lives? Hadn't she been the one who was always the center of attention on Easter Sunday?

Well, as it did every year, Spring came and so did Easter. As always, the children jumped out of bed and ran downstairs to see what was in their baskets. Phoebe was there by the baskets as she was every Easter morning. After a quick breakfast, they ate some of the chocolate bunnies from their Easter baskets and enjoyed some of the colored jelly beans.

Then the children started to get their playclothes on so the Easter egg hunt could begin. The snow had melted away this year so they were sure the hunt would take place outside. The children (and Phoebe) were very surprised when their parents told them the Easter egg hunt would have to wait. The parents told the children that they had decided to go to church this Easter.

The parents explained to the children they were sure there was more to Easter than eggs, bunnies, jelly beans, and Easter egg hunts.

Now the children were not happy about waiting until later for the Easter egg hunt; but, being obedient children, they got dressed for church. Poor Phoebe wanted to shout and cry, "What do you mean, Easter isn't about bunnies?" Phoebe worried and wrung her little bunny paws.

The family got all dressed up, and after the mother inspected each one to see that they looked just right, they left for church. Poor Phoebe—as soon as the door closed, tears began to well up in her little bunny eyes. Just when she thought her little heart would break, the door flew open and in rushed the oldest girl. She grabbed Phoebe by the arm and ran back out. Phoebe could hardly believe it; she was going to church, too!

As the family arrived at the church, looking quite nice in their new clothes, they felt a little nervous. A nice man came and showed them to a seat. Easter lilies decorated the church, and beautiful music filled the air. There was so much to see and hear that Phoebe and the children soon forgot to be afraid and began to look and listen to everything going on around them.

When the music stopped and it got very quiet, a man stood up in front of the people and began to tell everyone the wonderful truth about Easter. He told them God sent a Savior to the world. Then this Savior died and was placed in a tomb with a big stone rolled in front of it. He told them about how sad His friends were and how they thought all hope was lost. Then he told them this Savior came back to life because He was stronger than death. The man told them that when the Savior's friends saw He was alive, they were filled with hope and joy.

Best of all, the parents heard that this Savior knew them and their children by name, and He loved them and wanted to be their very best Friend. They heard that the Savior, whose name is Jesus, wanted to walk close to them. He wanted to teach them that He gave life to the earth when it looked dark and drab and dead. He was the One who caused the Winter to end and the Spring to come, the grass to grow, and the crocus and daffodil to push up through the hard ground. This Savior was the whole reason for Easter!

The family left church that day with their hearts full of joy and hope. For the first time, they understood what Easter really meant. Now they knew there was an even greater reason to celebrate Easter than they had ever imagined. As the family drove home, they talked about the wonderful things they had learned. They were excited and knew there was much more to learn about this Savior and His love for them.

But Phoebe the bunny was very concerned. Did this mean there wasn't going to be any more Easter baskets or Easter egg hunts? Would the family still love her and make her an important part of Easter, or would she find herself on a shelf deep in the basement?

Well, Phoebe didn't need to worry. As the years

passed, she continued to live in the main part of the house. She continued to sleep with the children; and each Easter morning, she sat by the Easter baskets. The Easter egg hunts continued, too. Phoebe was still a very important part of Easter—of course, not the most important part—but a very important part just the same. Whenever the family thought about Phoebe they were reminded of God's faithfulness and love for them.

Over the years, the children grew and life changed for the family. There were times of sickness, and times when the father didn't have work. The parents wondered how they would be able to care for their children. When they thought all hope was gone, they noticed Phoebe sitting nearby and remembered the hope that Easter brings. Phoebe reminded them that they had a Friend who was faithful and would meet all of their needs. And He always did!

The children grew to be adults and had children of their own. Now the parents had finally become grandparents. How they loved their grandchildren! Each one was precious and a great blessing to them.

Phoebe missed the children; she missed being able to watch over them as she had for so many years. But the grandchildren spent time at the grandparents' house and each one got to know Phoebe, and she got to know them. Even though she was getting old and a little worn, Phoebe was still a constant reminder of God's faithfulness and the promise of Easter. She helped the grandparents remember all the years of hope and faithfulness since learning the real meaning of Easter. But little did Phoebe know her greatest task of being a reminder of God's faithfulness was still ahead.

The little baby girl who was born that spring day all those years ago had grown up. She was married now and had a baby of her own. How the grandparents loved that grandchild! The day came when the little girl, who was now all grown up, had to move far away. She and her husband and the grandchild were moving far across the ocean.

The day they left, the grandparents thought their hearts would break. They felt as bad as the earth looks at the end of Winter. Just when everything looked hopeless, the grandparents noticed Phoebe sitting on the trunk, where she had been since the last grandchild had visited. Then the grandparents remembered the promise of Easter and the Friend and Savior who loved them. Their sadness was replaced with joy. They remembered that God had a special reason for their daughter to be exactly where she was. They knew He would help them face this difficult time.

God was indeed faithful. The grandparents were able to visit their daughter, who was now a mother with children of her own. As the years passed, the grandparents flew far across the ocean to visit her each time a new grandchild was added to her family.

One day the little boy, who had grown to be a man with children of his own, moved far away with his two children. Then the last little girl, who also became a mother, moved away, too. The grandparents were very sad and their hearts ached, but again they noticed Phoebe sitting in her place, and suddenly they remembered the promise of Easter and the faithfulness of God.

Phoebe and the grandparents learned very important lessons over the years. Phoebe learned she was not the most important part of Easter, but instead had a special job to remind the family of the promise of Easter and God's faithfulness.

The grandparents learned they could trust God to bring hope and joy, that He brought new life when everything around them looked dark. They also learned they could trust God to watch over their children and grandchildren no matter how far away they lived.

Phoebe still lives at the grandparents' house; she still waits and watches and is delighted when children and grandchildren come to visit; and she still reminds the grandparents of the promise of Easter—that God is always faithful.

MARGE ALEXANDER is a frequent speaker to women's groups. She has been delighting her grandcildren for many years with her unique stories. She and her husband live in Brattleboro, Vermont.

Other children's books from Evergreen Press

The Green Prophet (fiction)
One day, the Lord told Russ to give some special news to the city of Muddville. But would the people listen to a frog? Ages 5-9
ISBN 1-56043-243-8 16 pg. Softcover $3.95 retail

Who Am I?
This delightful book imparts to children a strong confidence in their heavenly Father and teaches them the truths about being a child of God. Ages 3-8
ISBN 1-58169-018-5 20 pg. Softcover $4.95 retail

The Truth About Santa Claus
Helps kids make the transition from "believing" in Santa to understanding the true meaning of Christmas. Ages 3-8
ISBN 1-56043-242-X 32 pg. Softcover $5.95 retail